For Marc and Dorine,
without whom this story wouldn't exist.

This book belongs to:

_____

Be nice to this book!

If you want to write to Felix,
send a postcard or letter with your name, age, and address to:
Friends of Felix, P. O. Box 5359, F.D.R. Station, New York, N.Y. 10150

Library of Congress Cataloging-in-Publication Data
available upon request

First published in English copyright © 1995 Abbeville Press.

ISBN 0-7892-0002-3

First edition
2 4 6 8 10 9 7 5 3 1

FELIX
TRAVELS BACK
IN TIME

**Includes Six Pull-out Letters
and Fold-out Map and Time Line**

Story by Annette Langen
Illustrations by Constanza Droop

ABBEVILLE KIDS
A DIVISION OF ABBEVILLE PUBLISHING GROUP
NEW YORK   LONDON   PARIS

Sophie

During a school field trip to the museum something strange happened: Sophie's cuddly rabbit Felix suddenly disappeared.

"Felix, where are you?" whispered Sophie, "come out right now!" But her little stuffed rabbit wasn't hiding in the old suit of armor. "Felix, stop hiding," Sophie called, now a little louder, as she searched underneath all the benches in the museum.

Felix wasn't there either!

"Don't worry, we'll find your Felix," Sophie's favorite teacher said, and she talked with the museum guard. He pushed his cap back from his forehead, put on his glasses, and began searching for Felix. But even though he and Sophie's entire class scoured the museum, the little rabbit and his backpack were nowhere to be found.

This was very, very bad! Sophie and
Felix had known each other forever, or
at least since they had snuggled together
in Sophie's crib. And even when Sophie grew bigger, Felix still
got to sleep in her bed. Sophie and the little cuddly rabbit were
inseparable. They were separated once, when Felix
went on a world tour. But he sent her letters from
everywhere and came back at
Christmas. Felix always
understood Sophie, and
Sophie understood Felix.

Outside the museum the bus driver honks his horn again and again to let the children know it's time to leave. There still isn't a trace of Felix. "Sophie, we really have to leave now," her teacher says gently. Sophie feels a lump in her throat. "Don't be sad, the museum guard has promised to call the minute Felix turns up!" Sophie can only nod in silence because she has to fight so hard to keep back the tears.

In the late afternoon Sophie returns home without Felix. Luckily Grandma is there. She doesn't ask any questions and makes a hot chocolate for Sophie and then tea for herself. Sophie drinks a big gulp, and then another, and then the tears begin to roll down her cheeks. Grandma hands Sophie one of her nicest handkerchiefs and takes her into her arms.

After a few sobs, Sophie tells the story: about the museum and the knight's armor, which was empty, about the big search and the nice museum guard. . . .

Grandma listens to every word while it grows pitch black outside. "Now," she says quietly, "there are more things between heaven and earth than we imagine." Sophie looks into the starry sky. "Where can Felix be now?" she thinks, and she whispers, "Do you think he's all right?" "Of course he is," Grandma says with a smile. "He's already traveled around the world, so we know he can take care of himself." Mom and Dad say exactly the same thing as soon as they're home from shopping. Only a little reassured, but very tired, Sophie falls asleep.

The next day Sophie's dad wakes her up to show her a crumpled letter from Felix that mysteriously appeared at the museum.

SOMEONE PLEASE
BRING THIS MESSAGE
TO MY DEAR
SOPHIE
33 ELM ROAD
MANSFIELD, OHIO

Sophie's heart sinks. Felix has never been so far away from home!
How could she help him? Perplexed, Sophie looks at the letter. Poor
Felix could freeze in the Stone Age—maybe even starve! There might
not even have been carrots then, and he loves carrots so much. Sophie
shuffles sadly around the house. Dad asks: "What does Felix say,
Sophie?" Without a word she hands him the letter. "Hmm, well,
that's something," Dad mumbles, and Sophie grows more
worried. "Dad," Sophie asks, "when exactly was the
Stone Age—was it 1,000 years ago?" "Oh, no,"
Dad says, "it's been 15,000 years
since the time of the cave men."
Sophie thinks that's awfully far
away and wonders how Felix
can return.

After lunch Sophie and Julius sneak out the back door and set off for a nearby cave. In a bag they bring two paint sets, a flashlight, and Julius's favorite book about the Stone Age.

Later that afternoon Sophie and her brother take their sister Lena, their brother Nicolas, and Mom and Dad hiking and lead them to the cave. Inside it is cool, and in the light of the flashlight they discover pictures on the walls.

"Wow," Mom says, "did you guys know that real cave men live in our neighborhood?" Her voice echoes through the cave and suddenly an owl flies past. "Eeeek!" Lena cries, and Dad is so scared that he drops his flashlight.

Sophie doesn't hear again from Felix for a while, but then a blue envelope addressed to Sophie is found in the museum. Mom goes to get the letter, and Sophie is overjoyed.

P. 16〈美〉

discus thrower

Parthenon

Athena

Sophie finishes the letter. She can't read it again, because this evening she gets to spend the night with Grandma. She quickly packs her backpack and sticks the letter from Felix in her pocket. Then she rides her bike to Grandma's house. She comes in out of breath, and Grandma gives her ice cream and cookies. Then Grandma reads the letter. "Did Felix make up what he says about the Olympics?" Sophie asks and looks at Grandma. "Oh, my, no," says Grandma, "he is absolutely correct about that." She gets up and finds a thick book. "The Greeks staged those games in honor of Zeus, the father of their gods, and what Felix described was a discus thrower!"

It's true, in Grandma's book there are photos of painted vases and plates with drawings of athletes on them. Sophie had never thought that plates could tell so much about the past!

Aphrodite

Zeus

Demeter

Poseidon

Hermes

Grandma explains that there are scientists who have gone to places where great cities once stood, and they dug up and pieced together ancient objects, from cups to buildings. "And that's how," Sophie marvels, "we know how people lived thousands of years ago!" Sophie looks through the book for a long time. The Greeks even had a whole family of gods! She especially likes a god with wings on his feet, named Hermes. He was supposed to work as the messenger of the gods and protect travelers. She hopes this Hermes will also make sure that her Felix gets home safe and sound! Tonight Sophie is allowed to stay up a long time, and she and Grandma sit on the porch and talk. Suddenly Grandma exclaims, "Oh, look, a shooting star! Quick, make a wish!" Sophie does, and she hopes that her wish will soon be granted.

The following week a man comes to the schoolyard to see Sophie. She recognizes him right away: it's the museum guard, and he's carrying a letter for her in his hand.

PLEASE DELIVER THIS ✉
TO
SOPHIE
33 ELM ROAD
MANSFIELD, OHIO

The school bell rings. With the letter in her hand Sophie runs into the classroom so fast that she almost bumps into her favorite teacher! "Whoops! Not so fast," her teacher says and asks softly: "Well, has there been any news from Felix?" Sophie shows her the letter: "It's all so strange—Felix writes about people with pots on their heads!" "What a coincidence," Sophie's teacher says with surprise, "Today I was planning to tell you about the Vikings!"

Viking long ship

And then she does. Sophie learns that the Vikings lived long ago on seacoasts in Scandinavia, were exceptional shipbuilders and sailors, and had even landed in America before Columbus!

"Oh, how wonderful it would be," Sophie thinks, "if Felix would sail back to me in one of those ships."

That weekend Sophie goes with Dad to the museum, but no matter how hard they search, they cannot find a new letter from Felix. Sophie stands by the Stone Age exhibit for a long time. "Come home, Felix," Sophie whispers sadly. On the way home Dad holds her hand. At the house there is a surprise. Lying in the yard are all the planks to build a Viking ship! Everybody pitches in: Julius sews a striped bed sheet into a sail, Lena finds two helmets on the attic floor, and Nicolas looks in the basement for a paint bucket. In pretty letters Sophie paints the name VIKING I. When the ship is finally ready, they invite Mom and Dad to the christening. Afterward, Sophie and her brothers and sister set sail!

A few weeks later Sophie goes back to the museum with her mom. They can't find Felix anywhere, but there on the floor lies a colorful envelope!

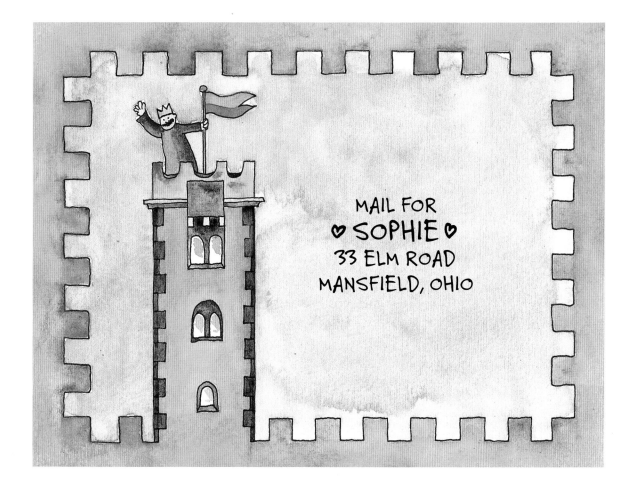

MAIL FOR
♡ SOPHIE ♡
33 ELM ROAD
MANSFIELD, OHIO

minstrels

guard

Sophie reads the letter twice right away. She can hardly believe that Felix has written her again. "Mom, just look!" she calls, "another letter from my Felix!"

Mom takes a look at the letter and is amazed.

"It sounds like Felix has landed in the Middle Ages." Sophie looks closely at the old pictures. There's one with a knight on a horse and a castle in the background—just like Felix described in his letter! Astounded, Sophie whispers, "How did Felix get to the Middle Ages?" And she wonders how Felix can come back to the twentieth century from the Middle Ages. Mom doesn't know the answer to that question, but she does know someone who is an expert on the Middle Ages—the museum director.

"Anybody who has so many books, pictures, and maps must really know what's what," Sophie thinks a little later. She wonders if the museum director actually lives in his office. "Ah, yes," he says, "the splendor of the Middle Ages . . . see for yourself!"

Sophie loses track of time as the director spreads out plans of old castles. There is a watchtower, supply rooms, and way down at the bottom Sophie can see a dungeon. "But do you know what a 'privy' was?" he asks with a grin as he points out a small structure above the circular wall. There, high in the air, was the bathroom. Sophie definitely has to tell Lena, Julius, and Nicolas about this!

Two weeks later the old museum guard appears again with another letter from Felix. Sophie opens the envelope anxiously and begins to read.

IMPORTANT NEWS FOR
SOPHIE
33 ELM ROAD
MANSFIELD, OHIO

P. 28 〈美〉

Sophie is absolutely certain that Felix is in Japan, and that's what Aunt Edda, who's come to visit, thinks too. "Did you know that Asia is known as 'the cradle of technology?'" she asks. "Imagine, Sophie, the magnetic compass, the art of

printing, and much more were invented there centuries earlier than in Europe!" Sophie fishes around in her pocket and proudly pulls out the card with the characters. "Your Felix has already learned a lot," says Aunt Edda in amazement. She says there are thousands of characters used for writing in Japan, and each of them has a special meaning!

"Oh, dear, I hope Felix won't learn them all," Sophie mumbles sadly, "or I'll be a great-grandmother by the time he comes back!"

Hōryū-ji temple

That day Sophie and her family decide to have a Japanese meal—with lots of rice, of course! Aunt Edda and Sophie go shopping together and even find real chopsticks. Then Aunt Edda disappears into the kitchen, and soon it smells delicious! And it tastes delicious too. Only Dad struggles desperately with his chopsticks and exclaims, "This is too complicated!" Lena laughs and then comforts him, "Don't worry, Dad, we won't let you starve!" Relieved, Dad sighs: "It's a good thing we're going to the Great Lakes for our summer vacation. If we went to Japan I might starve!"

After supper Aunt Edda has to leave, and everybody waves from the gate until her car is too far away to see.

Just when Sophie has almost lost all hope of receiving news from Felix, a call comes from the museum! They have found a new envelope addressed in Felix's writing.